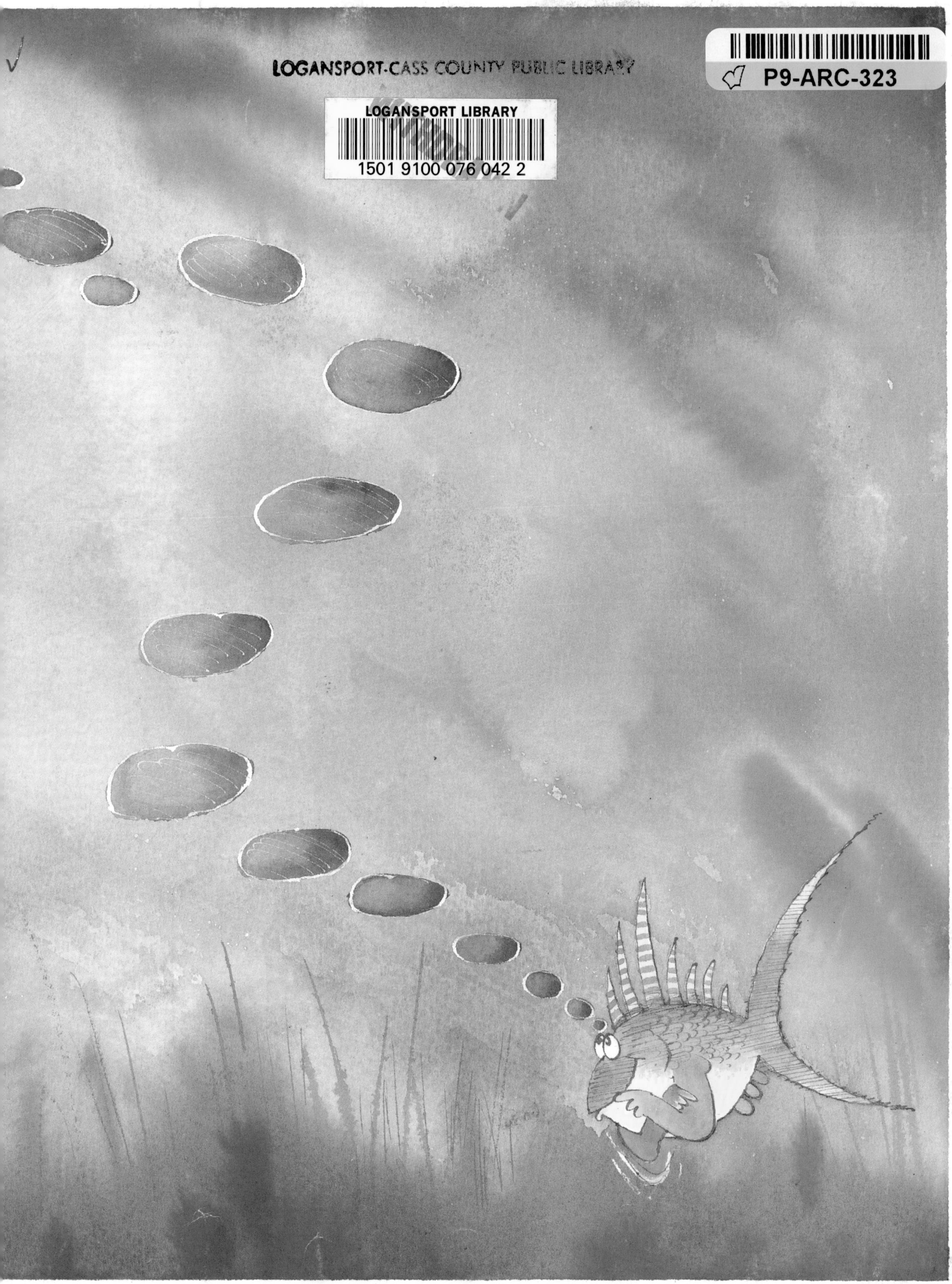

For Carl and Kerri-Leigh
JB

For the Tzannes family
KP

First American Edition 1991 by Kane/Miller Book Publishers
Brooklyn, New York & La Jolla, California

Originally published in England in 1991 by Oxford University Press
Text copyright © John Bush 1991
Illustrations copyright © Korky Paul 1991

Library of Congress Cataloging-in-Publication Data

Bush, John.
The fish who could wish / John Bush & Korky Paul. — 1st American
ed.
p.   cm.
Summary: A fish's wishes come true until the day he makes a
foolish wish.
ISBN 0-916291-35-9
[1. Fishes—Fiction.   2. Wishes—Fiction.   3. Stories in rhyme.]
I. Paul, Korky.   II. Title.
PZ8.3.B975F1   1991
[E]—dc20   90-46667
                                                            CIP
                                                            AC

Printed in Singapore by Tien Wah Press Pte. Ltd.

2 3 4 5 6 7 8 9 10

THE FISH
who could wish

JOHN BUSH & KORKY PAUL

A CRANKY NELL BOOK

KM Kane/Miller Book Publishers

Brooklyn, New York & La Jolla, California

In the deep blue sea,
In the deep of the blue,
Swam a fish who could wish,
And each wish would come true.
Oh the fun that he had!
Oh the things he would do!
Just wishing away
In the deep water blue.

500054

He wished for a castle.

He wished for a car.

He wished for a horse
And a Spanish guitar.

Once, when he wished
He could go out and ski
It snowed for a week
Under the sea.

He wished he could fly
And to his delight,
Flew twice round the world
In exactly one night!

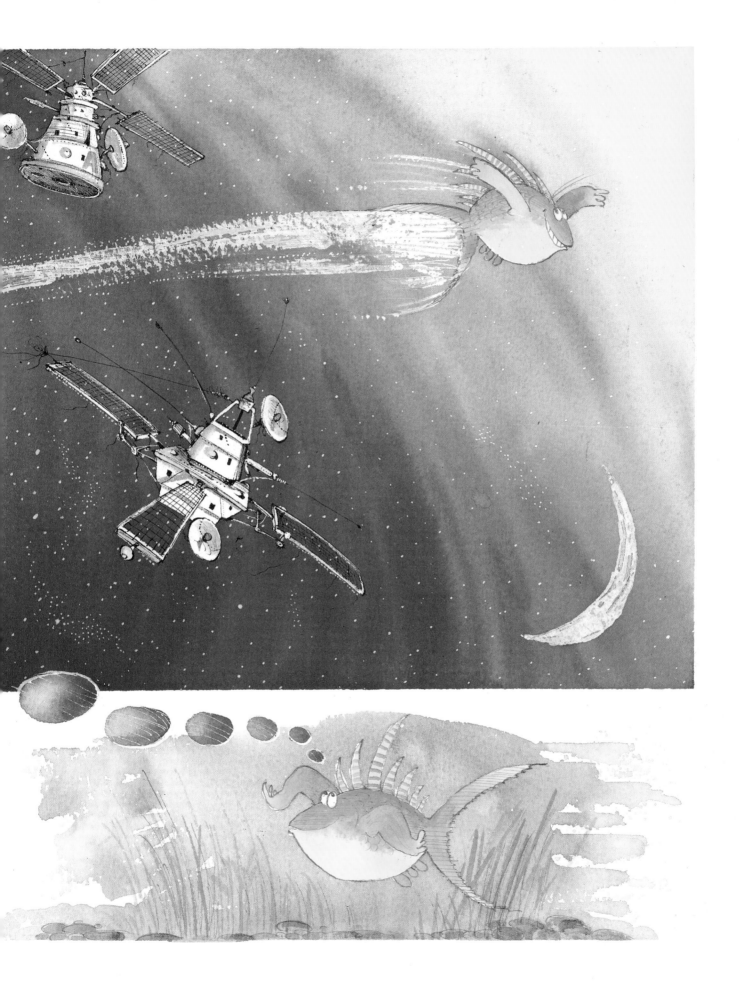

If sharks came a-hunting
For a nice fishy treat,
He'd quickly just wish
He was too small to eat.

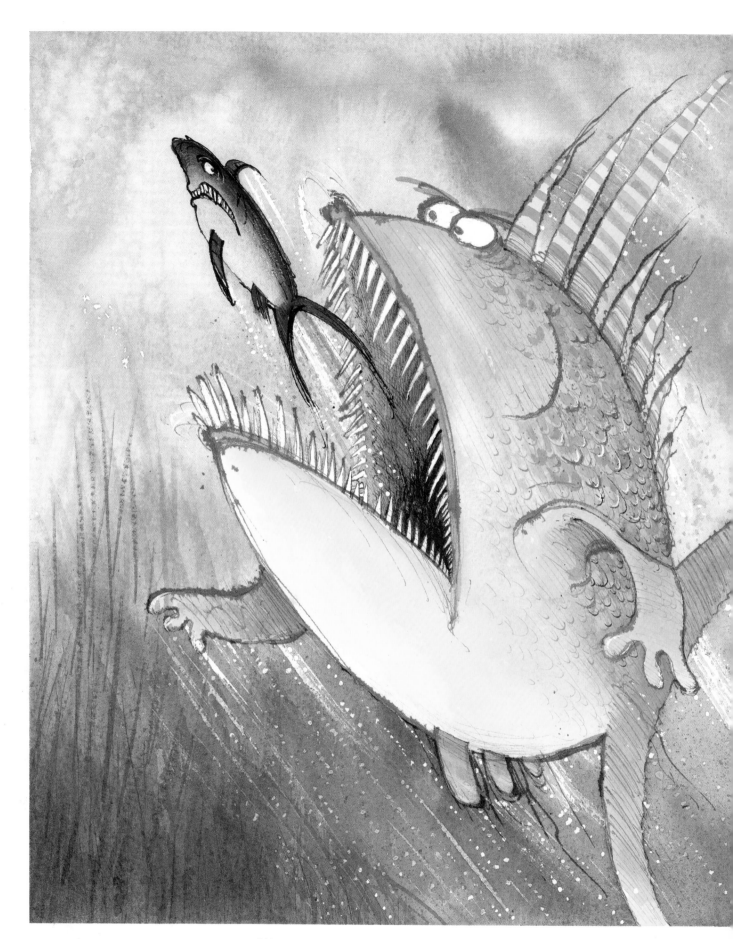

And to teach sharks a lesson,
Do you know what he'd wish?
That he was a shark
And the shark was a fish!

He'd wish himself square,
Or round as a biscuit,
Triangular, oval . . .
Name it, he wished it.

He wished for fine suits
And handsome silk ties,
But the one thing he never wished
Was to be wise . . .

One day, just for fun,
That silly old fish
Wished the silliest, silliest
Wish he could wish.

That silly old fish
Wished he could be
Just like all the other
Fish in the sea.
But wishing was something
Other fish could not do.
So that was his very last
wish that came true.